Everyone knows how a day goes.

The sun rises and shines above us
with his glorious smile.

At the end of the day,
he disappears over the horizon.

But what people don't know
is what the sun gets up to
after he goes home . . .

For my brother
M.A.

ORCHARD BOOKS

First published in Great Britain in 2021 by The Watts Publishing Group

1 3 5 7 9 10 8 6 4 2

Text and illustrations © Momoko Abe 2021

The moral rights of the author-illustrator have been asserted.

A CIP catalogue record for this book is available from the British Library.

HB ISBN 978 1 40835 832 0
PB ISBN 978 1 40835 831 3

Printed and bound in China

MIX
Paper from responsible sources
FSC
www.fsc.org
FSC® C104740

Orchard Books
An imprint of Hachette Children's Group
Part of The Watts Publishing Group Limited
Carmelite House, 50 Victoria Embankment, London EC4Y 0DZ

An Hachette UK Company
www.hachette.co.uk
www.hachettechildrens.co.uk

WHEN THE SUN GOES HOME

Momoko Abe

ORCHARD

Every day, from dawn till dusk, the sun shone
high in the sky, smiling his **very best smile.**

He knew people loved to see him, and
he worked hard to make them happy.

At the end of each day, the
sun made a wonderful sunset.
Then he handed the sky over to
the moon, before going back
to his home beyond the horizon.

When the sun got home . . .

he ate his dinner . . .

did a jigsaw puzzle . . .

. . . then he practised his smile so it would
be extra-specially bright the next day.

"I must keep up the good work,"
he said to himself. "My smile
HAS to be perfect."

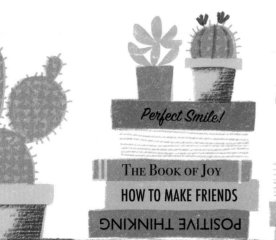

HOW TO SMILE

13 STEPS TO
HAPPINESS

The Shining

THE ART OF HAPPINESS

The POWER of SMILE

SMILE for LIFE

Perfect Smile!

THE BOOK OF JOY

HOW TO MAKE FRIENDS

POSITIVE THINKING

And for a
long time,
that's how
things went.

What nobody realised was that beneath the sun's bright smile, he didn't **always** feel so sunny.

It was lonely up there in the sky.

If **only** someone would smile back at him!

But they never did.

How lucky the moon is, thought the sun.
She always has the stars for company.

I wish *I* had a friend.

Spring turned to summer.
Every day, the sun shone high in the
sky. But as he watched people having
fun below, he began to feel sad.

I think I'll go home early
today, he thought to himself.
It doesn't really matter.
No one notices me anyway.

Smiling was just **too hard.**

But the next morning, the moon came to knock on the sun's door. "Because **you** left so early yesterday, **I** had to look after the sky for longer," she said angrily.

"Come out, Sun! It's time to start shining. Everyone is counting on **you.**"

The sun felt heavy inside. The moon is right, he thought.
I HAVE to smile.

So the sun went
back to the sky.

and smiled . . .

He took a deep breath . . .

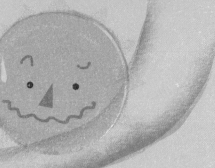

and smiled . . .

and smiled.

"I must keep smiling,"
he said to himself.

"I must keep SMILING."

But as he smiled and **shone**, the sun began to feel too **hot.**

Then he started to feel very **tired.** Everything around him was **spinning.**

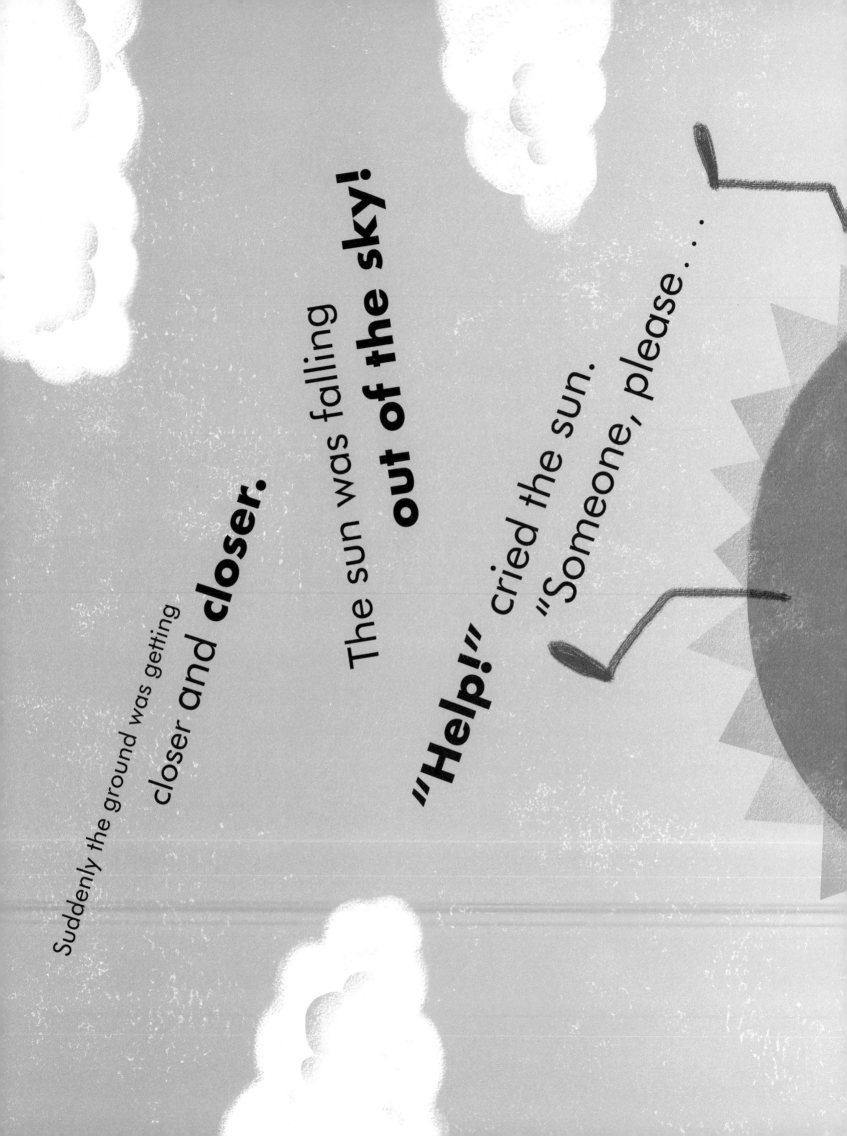

Suddenly the ground was getting closer and **closer.**

The sun was falling **out of the sky!**

"Help!" cried the sun. "Someone, please...."

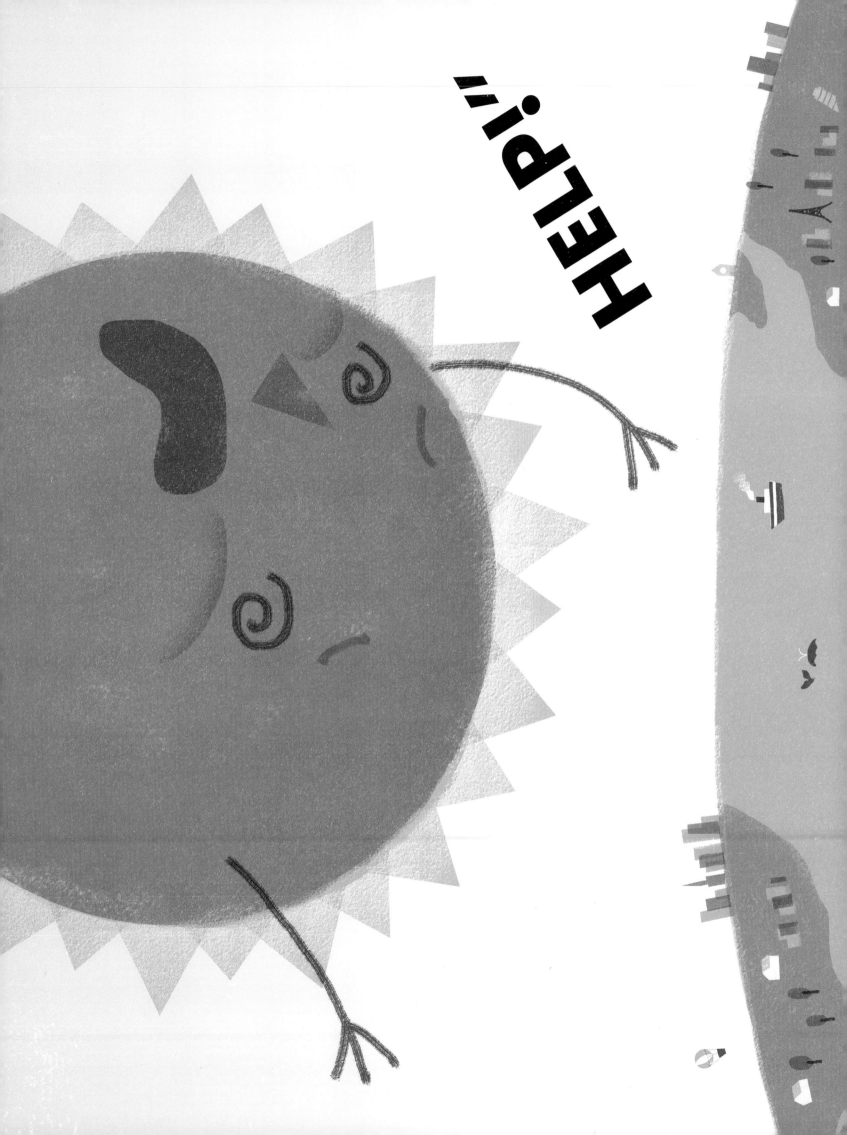

Then, all of a sudden, the sun felt
cool, soft cushions beneath him.

"We've got you," said the clouds.
"Get some rest while we rain."

"But I can't let everyone down!" cried the sun.
"I have to shine. I have to SMILE!"

"No one can smile all the time,"
said the clouds. "People need rain just as
much as they need sunshine. Trust us."

So while the clouds rained, the sun closed his eyes and rested. He felt a gentle breeze on his burning cheeks, and inside he felt warm **and happy.**
No one had ever cared about him like this before.

And it wasn't long before the sun felt ready
to shine again. He thanked the clouds,
and as they drifted away, he smiled
his big, glorious smile . . .

which met with the rain
and made . . .

a RAINBOW!

The sun was still
smiling that night when he
handed the sky over to the moon.

"Goodnight, Sun," said the moon, smiling
back at him. "Did you have a good day?"

"A very good day,
thank you, Moon," said the sun.

And as the stars twinkled goodnight, he
went home feeling **very happy.**

And now, whenever
he doesn't feel so sunny,
the sun knows just what to do . . . .

The end